Bones

Best Friends Series
Book 1

David M. Sargent, Jr. and his friends all live in a small town in northwest Arkansas. While he lies in the hammock, the dogs (left to right: Spike, Emma, Daphne and Mary) play ball, dig holes or bark at kitty cats. When not playing in the yard, they travel around the United States, meeting children and writing stories.

Bones

Best Friends Series
Book 1

David M. Sargent, Jr.

Illustrated by Debbie Farmer

Ozark Publishing, Inc.
P.O. Box 228
Prairie Grove, AR 72753

Cataloging-in-Publication Data

Sargent, David M., 1966–
    Bones / by David M. Sargent, Jr. ;
illustrated by Debbie Farmer.—Prairie Grove, AR :
Ozark Publishing, c2007.
    p. cm. (Best friends series ; 1)

    "Hidden talent"—Cover.
    SUMMARY: When a neighbor's young girl
disappears, Seth helps look for her. When they
can't find her, they call the police. Bones
discovers one of the little girl's dolls in the
front yard. He sniffs it, gets her scent and takes off!
    ISBN 1-59381-054-7 (hc)
           1-59381-055-5 (pbk)

    1. Dogs—Juvenile fiction.
[1. Dogs—Fiction. 2. Bloodhound—Fiction.]
I. Farmer, Debbie, 1958– ill. II. Title.
III. Series.

    PZ8.3.S2355Bo 2007
    [E]—dc21   2003099195

Printed in the United States of America

Inspired by

David's grandpa who had a dog named Bones. Bones was a Bloodhound. Everyone thought Bones was just worthless until he became a hero.

Dedicated to

all children who have *special* dogs.

Foreword

When a neighbor's young girl disappears, Seth helps look for her. When they can't find her, they call the police. Bones discovers one of the little girl's dolls in the front yard. He sniffs it. Good! He has her scent! He takes off!

Contents

One   A Worthless Bloodhound   1

Two   A Missing Child   9

Three   A Real Hero!   17

If you would like to have the author of the Best Friends Series visit your school free of charge, please call 1-800-321-5671.

One

A Worthless Bloodhound

Seth tossed the ball across the yard and yelled, "Go get it, Bones!"

Bones just sat there. Happily wagging his tail, he looked at the boy, then glanced toward the ball and stood up.

He licked Seth's hand with his big wet tongue, then sat back down.

"Bones," Seth scolded, "can't you do anything right? You just hang around and want me to pet you. You're not good for anything!" Bones lowered his head.

Seth grumbled as he walked across the yard to pick up the ball. Suddenly he heard Mrs. Jenkins, his next door neighbor, calling his name.

"Seth, is Mandy with you? She was here in our yard a moment ago, but now I can't find her."

"No, Mrs. Jenkins. I haven't seen her all morning," Seth replied.

"Oh dear me," the lady groaned. "Where could that little girl be? She was playing right here only minutes ago."

Seth smiled and said, "She can't be far, Mrs. Jenkins. I'll help you find her."

Two

A Missing Child

An hour passed with Seth and Mrs. Jenkins searching the entire neighborhood for the missing child.

Bones followed at the boy's heels as they walked down each street, calling the little girl's name. When they got home, Mrs. Jenkins burst into tears.

"I'm going to call the police, Seth. I thought we'd find her playing with one of her little friends. Where could...." The woman was crying too hard to finish the statement.

A tear slid down the boy's cheek as he watched the lady run inside to telephone the police. Bones whined and laid down beside him.

Minutes later, the wail of a very loud siren was heard. The police car came to a quick stop in front of the house.

Two men in uniforms talked with Mrs. Jenkins. Seth and Bones stood nearby and watched as the lady showed them a picture of Mandy.

Suddenly Bones walked over to a doll that was lying on the grass in the front yard. He sniffed it several times, then looked at Seth.

"Hey, look at that Bloodhound. He's getting her scent," one of the policemen said.

All eyes turned toward the big dog.

Three

A Real Hero!

The policemen looked at Seth. "Is that your Bloodhound, Son?"

"Yessir," Seth replied. "But he isn't much account. He doesn't do anything but eat and sleep. He just wants to be petted. I call him Bones."

"Maybe you should give him a chance, Son," the policeman said. He walked over to Bones and picked up the doll.

He held it up for Bones to sniff and then said, "Go find her, Bones. Come on, Boy. Let's find Mandy."

Bones wagged his tail, then threw his head back and howled. He ran from the yard with his nose close to the ground. Seth, Mrs. Jenkins, and the policeman followed.

A short time later, Bones was darting among the trees in the woods. Suddenly he stopped and wagged his tail.

A child was sitting beside the tree, crying. Bones licked her face.

"It's Mandy!" Seth yelled. "Bones found Mandy!"

Mandy ran to her mother, and Seth hugged Bones.

"You're a good dog, Bones, and I love you! You're my best friend."